Date Due

DEC 1 3 1983		
NOV 10 '90		
NOV 25 '93		

THE
PERFECT PITCH

To Tommy

THE
PERFECT PITCH

by Beman Lord

with a new introduction by the author

pictures by Harold Berson

GREGG PRESS
A DIVISION OF G. K. HALL & CO., BOSTON, 1981

Republished in 1981 by Gregg Press, A Division of G.K. Hall & Co., 70 Lincoln St., Boston, Massachusetts 02111.

First Printing, January, 1981

Library of Congress Cataloging in Publication Data

Lord, Beman.
    The perfect pitch.

    (Gregg Press children's literature series)
    Reprint of the ed. published by H. Z. Walck, New York.
    SUMMARY: A Little League baseball player who has trouble controlling his pitches meets an unusual man in the woods who gives him some magical help.
    [1. Baseball—Fiction. 2. Magic—Fiction]
I. Title. II. Series.
[PZ7.L877Pe 1981]   [Fic]   80-24624
ISBN 0-8398-2724-5

Introduction

A LL MY LIFE I HAVE HAD A SECRET FANTASY WHICH WILL NEVER BE fulfilled. I have always wanted the power to avoid being tackled as I run the length of the football field to score the goal that wins the game. In basketball, I crave the ability never to miss the basket. Naturally, in baseball, I want to pitch the perfect game. Some of my frustrations were eased when I wrote *The Perfect Pitch* (1965). But not all of them! I still want to be a sports hero.

When I was growing up we had lots of heroes to emulate—among them Ted Williams, Mickey Mantle, and Joe DiMaggio (I even admired his brother, Dom). Who wouldn't want to be like Ernie Calvelry, the short Rhode Island basketball player who shot a basket from center court to win the game as the final buzzer sounded? Incidentally, I saw that game which I suppose has only added to my desires.

In today's sports, where are all the heroes? Can one admire the great boxer who did everything to avoid the draft, or the great quarterback who was known more for his completed passes off the field than on? How about temperamental tennis stars who lose their cool in almost every match? Who can respect an outfielder whose ego seems to outshine his great hitting and fielding?

Much of this attitude seems to be carried over in our sports fiction of today. The main character often has so many problems that he is more ready for a psychiatrist's couch than he is to play third base.

The idea of a hero is, to me, not an old-fashioned idea whether in fiction or real life. How many times do you hear someone say, "Gee, when I grow up, I'd like to be...like...." We all must have goals, something to work for and someone we can pattern our life after. I believe the lack of heroes is the cause of many problems facing today's youth. Who can they follow?

I have admitted my impossible dream but that does not really stop it, dissipate it, nor discourage the hope that it may come true. Realistically I know it won't but, just maybe, it might. Dreams and heroes are something to have and aspire for always. Of course one must work for them as nothing comes easily. It must also be fun. The old saying comes to mind—"All work and no play makes Jack a dull boy."

In the story, I have touched on these points—hope, work, and a sense of humor—and I try not to lose sight of them in my daily life. Just maybe I will put on enough weight to play football, get perfect vision to sink the basket or throw perfect pitches. I would also have to regain my youth. Who knows, I may yet be a hero.

Beman Lord
New York City

Contents

1. Trouble on the Mound

It was the first game of the season. Tommy was nervous. He stood on the pitcher's mound and rubbed the ball in his mitt. "It's always the first batter," he thought. "Get him out of the way and then you'll settle down." He chewed his gum a little faster.

"Play ball," the umpire called, and the first batter stepped into the box.

Tommy went into his windup and threw. It was outside for a ball. The next pitch was fouled off.

"Now we have him swinging," Ted Roberts called from third. "Let him hit; we'll get him out."

On the third pitch the batter hit a grounder to second, who threw to first for an easy out.

Tommy sighed with relief. "If they all would be that easy, we'd have this game over in no time flat."

Unfortunately they weren't all that simple. Tommy got through the first three innings without too much trouble, but in the fourth the sky fell in. He walked the first man, and then a double and an error brought the runner home. That upset him, and before he could settle down again three runs crossed the plate. The Cards lost 4 to o.

"I'm sorry, coach," Tommy said after the game.

"Don't worry about it. The first game of a season is always the hardest. We'll win the next one," Mr. Ottoway said.

But Tommy couldn't stop worrying. He had let the team down. Instead of going home, he climbed the hill opposite his house and went into the woods. He had a favorite spot, by a little brook that was fed by an underground spring. He always went there, whenever he had things on his mind. He sat down on a rock and pounded his glove hard. "Of all the luck. Jumping Grasshoppers!" he said.

Suddenly he heard a voice behind him. "Yes, yes. What is it?"

Tommy jumped up with a start and turned around. There stood a tall, thin, odd-looking man dressed in a business suit with a vest and carrying a cane. "Holy smoke," Tommy said, "I didn't know anybody was here." He laughed. "You really gave me a scare."

"I'm sorry," the man said. "Allow me to introduce myself. My name is Henry Watts." He gave a little bow.

"Mine is Tommy Gans."

"Now that we know each other," Mr. Watts said, "what is it? I don't have too much time."

"What is what?" Tommy asked.

"You said the magic words. That means

you have a wish coming, and it looks to me as if you could use one. You look pretty sad. Now, what is it?"

Tommy didn't really know what this man was talking about. He seemed to be a nice person even though he was talking in riddles. And where did he come from? He was a stranger in town, for Tommy had never seen

him before. Also he talked with some kind of accent.

"Come, come. What is the problem?" Mr. Watts said. "Why are you looking as if you had lost your best friend?"

"The Cards lost today. I blew up. I was all right for the first three, and then they got to me. It was that double and then the error that did it. I wish no one could hit my pitches!"

He gave his glove another good pound.

The man looked at Tommy. "I don't know what you are saying, young man, but the wish is granted. Now if you will excuse me, I must get back to work. I have just been transferred to this area, and the last person in charge really left the place in a mess. Wishes that shouldn't have been granted, wishes half granted, and no follow-up on wishes. In fact, nothing done. Good-by and good luck."

Tommy listened in amazement, and stared at Mr. Watts. A noise behind him caused him to turn his head, and when he turned back the man was gone. "What a nut," he said and suddenly felt better. He had gotten things off his chest. He picked up his mitt and started home.

On Tuesday the Cards played the Mets. Tommy was sure he was going to pitch a good game. His arm felt looser. He threw two warm-up pitches that were a little wild and then had to take time out to fix the webbing in his glove, which had come loose. By the time he got it fixed the umpire had called, "Play ball."

He walked the first man and Ronnie Greenberg, who was playing catcher, came out to talk to him. "Settle down," he said. "Let them hit."

To the next batter Tommy threw four straight balls—one high, one low, one inside and one wide.

Ronnie walked to the mound again. "You're not watching my signals."

"I'm trying to," Tommy said. "But something happens when the ball leaves my glove."

The next batter also got a walk. One ball even went behind him and Ronnie had trouble catching it. The bases were loaded, and the coach put in a new pitcher.

"You weren't going to let anybody hit a ball, were you?" Mr. Ottoway said, when Tommy sat down on the bench. "What was wrong with your control today?"

"I'm sorry, coach," Tommy said. "I don't know what was happening out there. Every time I thought I was throwing a strike it turned out to be a ball."

All through the game Tommy tried to figure out what had gone wrong. Why hadn't he had any control? He was still thinking about it as he walked home. When he reached his house, he threw the glove on the porch and started to climb the hill slowly. Halfway up the hill he remembered the man. What had he said to him? Something about not wanting anybody to hit his pitches. Could Mr. Watts really grant wishes? Tommy started to run.

2. Letter-high and Perfect

When he reached the brook, he tried to remember his conversation. It was like trying to remember "Open Seasame!" He called, "Holy Smoke!" and nothing happened. What were those words? "Jumping Jupiter!" He was getting close. It was jumping, he was quite sure. What jumped? "Grasshoppers," he yelled. "Jumping Grasshoppers!" Mr. Watts appeared.

"It's you again. I'm extremely busy. I was way on the other side of town trying to..."

"Excuse me for interrupting but you can grant wishes, can't you?" Tommy asked.

"Of course I can," Mr. Watts said very sternly. "Didn't you get yours? If I remember correctly it was something about not wanting anyone to hit your pitches. You got your wish. I watched the game and saw to that."

"You misunderstood me," Tommy said. "All I threw were balls and everybody got a walk."

"It is good for everyone to take a walk. Doctors say so."

"But not in a baseball game," Tommy quickly added.

"I don't know anything about baseball. I was in England before I came here and they don't play the game over there. All I know is that you got your wish. Now you don't want it."

"I want strikes, not balls!" Tommy said
emphatically.

Mr. Watts thought for a minute.

"Usually we don't change wishes, but if I
misunderstood perhaps something can be

done. I'm frightfully busy today so I haven't too much time to discuss this with you. It seems my predecessor granted a wish for a lady to go to Saturn. We don't have any authority outside Earth. I've tried to explain this to her, but she won't listen to me. Now my problem is..."

"Excuse me for interrupting again. I know you have problems, but this is very important to me and the team. All I want is to throw perfect strikes and..."

"I know, I know. Wish granted. You will now throw only perfect strikes. Now I really must run. Good-by and good luck." Before Tommy could get to his feet, Mr. Watts had disappeared into the woods.

Tommy could hardly wait for the next

game. If Mr. Watts could really grant wishes, he would have nothing to worry about. His teammates would be pleased with him and he would be out of the doghouse for losing the last game.

"How is your control, today?" the coach asked, as they were taking batting practice before the game.

"Fine," Tommy said. "Everything I throw is going to be a strike."

And everything Tommy threw was a strike. A perfect strike, letter high. It was what every batter dreams of and every batter took advantage of it. The first player hit a double to left field. The second hit a triple to right field. The third got a single and the

fourth, batting in cleanup, cleaned up, all right, with a homer. The coach put in a new pitcher.

"What happened?" the coach asked, as Tommy took his place on the bench.

"I could only throw strikes," Tommy said weakly.

"It's fine to throw strikes," Mr. Ottoway said, "but they don't all have to be perfect letter-high pitches. Maybe next week you'll do better."

"I'd better," Tommy thought to himself. He wanted to see Mr. Watts right away. "Coach, I'm not feeling well. Could I leave the game?"

The coach looked at him. "You don't look too well to me. You'd better go home."

Tommy left the field running. He didn't stop until he was resting by the brook in the woods. He was so out of breath that he could only whisper, "Jumping Grasshoppers!" Nothing happened. After a few minutes he managed to say it aloud, and Mr. Watts appeared.

"You're here again? I was hoping I had seen the last of you. And why couldn't you wait until after the game was finished? I was just beginning to enjoy it. Now, what is the matter?"

"You fouled me up. They murdered me!
I was knocked out of the box! I faced four
men and they scored four runs!"

"Yes, wasn't it wonderful? It was such fun
to see everyone running and to see boys

standing on all those sacks. I was so pleased. As for knocking you out and murdering you, no one touched you. You're alive and have no bruises."

Tommy didn't know what to do. How could you talk to a guy like this? "You don't understand the game. I'm finished as a pitcher, thanks to you. You have no business granting wishes about something you don't know anything about. I want to talk to someone else. Someone who knows something about baseball!"

"Now let's not get hasty. Two men are never assigned to a wish. We are all too busy to talk in pairs to every Tommy, Dick and Harry. Granted I don't know the game, but you should be more careful with your wishes.

I repeated everything you said so there would be no misunderstanding this time."

Tommy just shook his head.

"Let us discuss this calmly and quietly. What exactly is it that you want?" Mr. Watts then sat down, and folded his hands.

"You really have me confused. I wished no one would hit my pitches, and they didn't. I wished for strikes, but how did I know they were going to be perfect strikes. Baseball isn't played that way." Tommy took a deep breath. "I'll try to explain it to you. I wish to throw only good balls and strikes. I want the other team not to hit or score any runs."

Mr. Watts took out a large handkerchief and wiped his face. "Now, I'm trying very carefully to get this straight. What you want is balls and strikes, but no hits or runs. Is that correct?"

"Yes," Tommy said.

"Wish granted," Mr. Watts said.

"Oh, no," Tommy yelled. "Not yet. I thought we were just talking it over. Take it back. I don't know what I wished for."

"I'm sorry, but the wish will have to stay," Mr. Watts said. "I've already exceeded my limit with you. Your wish was that you want balls and strikes, but no hits or runs. Now, I really must go. My supervisor is asking for action on that lady's wish to go to Saturn. Good-by and good luck."

Tommy didn't even watch him leave. He just sat there. What was going to go wrong this time? "What a mess," he groaned.

Tommy was depressed for the rest of the day, but when he was going to bed a thought crossed his mind. If he gave up no runs or hits and threw good balls and strikes, that would mean only one thing. Tommy went to bed feeling very happy.

3. The Last Inning

The day of the game, Tommy started against the Braves and he pitched just what he thought he would—a perfect game. The only trouble was that the Cards didn't score either and the game finally had to be called after ten innings.

By the time he climbed the hill, it was

slowly getting dark. He wondered why he felt so sad. Here he had pitched a perfect game and everybody had congratulated him but somehow he felt let down. Why? He sat by the brook and didn't say anything. "Any other pitcher would be on cloud nine after pitching a perfect game," he thought. "Why aren't I happy about it?" After about ten minutes of thinking he said, "Jumping Grasshoppers!"

"I've been expecting you for the last half hour," Mr. Watts said when he appeared. "As soon as the game was over I came right back here. It was a wonderful game. Aren't you pleased?"

Tommy just looked at him. "Sure," he said not very happily.

"You certainly don't look it," Mr. Watts said.

All Tommy could say was, "We didn't win."

"That was not part of the wish," Mr. Watts said. "I did exactly what you told me to do. The wish didn't ask for your team to win." Mr. Watts took out his handkerchief and blew his nose. "I'm beginning to feel a little hurt."

"I'm sorry," Tommy said. "It's really not your fault that you don't know the game. That's why the wishes have gotten all mixed up."

"Exactly. If they played cricket here, I could really help you."

Tommy stood up. "You still can help, can't you?"

"We really are not supposed to grant so many wishes to one person; but I guess we can change the rule this one time. There was misunderstanding, I can always say, if I am questioned."

"Gee thanks, Mr. Watts."

"However, you can't have the wish until I get Miss May and her wish to go to Saturn out of the way. Orders from higher up."

"That's fine by me," Tommy said. "I really didn't want the wish today anyway. I want to think about it before I tell you what it is. In the meantime, maybe you can learn more about the game."

"I'm sorry. I won't have time for that. I have got to concentrate full time on Miss May. Otherwise I may lose my job." Mr. Watts looked at Tommy. "You don't by chance know this woman, do you?"

Tommy nodded his head. "In the wintertime I keep her sidewalks clean and empty her ashes. She's a nice old lady."

"That's just the trouble. She is just too old and set in her ways. I can't reason with her. I'm afraid I have made her angry. Perhaps you could help me out and talk to her," Mr. Watts said very winningly.

Tommy started to say no and then decided that that was the least he could do for Mr. Watts. Anyway, he wouldn't be able to get his wish until her wish was cleared up. "All right, what do you want me to say?"

For the next twenty minutes they discussed the problem. By the time Tommy got back to his house it was almost dark and it was time for supper. After he had finished he walked up the street to Miss May's house.

Miss May lived by herself. In the wintertime she closed all of the house except her bedroom and kitchen. "It's easier to heat," she said. Tommy emptied the ashes from her stove and filled cereal boxes full of coal. "Easier to handle that way," Miss May said. She was at least eighty, he was sure, because she remembered the Spanish-American War clearly. Some people thought she was odd, but Tommy liked her and they got along very well. He knocked on the door.

"Why, it's Tommy Gans. How nice of you to call," Miss May said, when she opened the door. "Come in and let me hear all your

news." She took a pile of newspapers off a chair and put them on a table. "Sit right there so I can look at you."

Tommy did as he was told.

"I see by the paper you are playing baseball again this year. Having a little tough luck getting going, I also see. What seems to be the matter?"

"That's just what I want to talk to you about," Tommy said excitedly. "It's a Mr. Watts. I believe you know him."

"I should say I do. I liked the man before him much better. This man says he can do nothing about my wish. A wish is a wish, I always say. What has he done to you?"

Tommy told her the entire story. "So you

can see nothing will be done about my problem until yours is out of the way."

"Well, I certainly don't want anybody to lose his job, but all he keeps saying is the wish can't be granted. He says he knows nothing about outer space. Ignorance, that's what it is."

"Why do you want to go to Saturn, anyway?" Tommy asked.

"Everybody else is going to the moon and Mars, and I thought I could be the first to Saturn." She leaned closer to Tommy and said almost in a whisper, "You know, I've always liked those rings."

Tommy looked at her in amazement. "You wouldn't if you were there. Those rings are made up of ammonia and methane."

Miss May gasped. "You don't mean it! What else do you know about it? I've been meaning to read a few books on the subject, but I haven't gotten around to it yet. Tell me more."

"It's the second biggest planet in our solar system. The revolution around the sun takes almost thirty years. Its density is less than the Earth, although it weighs more." Tommy stopped for a minute and tried to remember other facts, but he couldn't. "Do you realize it would take you years to get there?"

"Why, I had never thought about that." She pulled her chair a little closer. "You know, what I really wanted was to travel fast."

"Why, you can do that in a jet. Have you ever been up in a plane?"

"I'm afraid I haven't, and I have always wanted to."

"Well, there's your wish. You could take a vacation."

"I'll go to Miami Beach. I've always wanted to go there. I won't even have to repack, for I was planning on taking only summer clothes to Saturn." Miss May was getting excited. "Jumping Grasshoppers!" she said, and Mr. Watts opened the door.

"You called?" he said, and bowed.

Miss May was quite surprised. "I hadn't meant to, but I was getting so excited. You will be happy to know that plans have been changed. I wish to go to Miami Beach, not Saturn."

"Thank goodness," Mr. Watts said. "Just

give me time to make reservations. Wish granted." He took out his handkerchief and wiped his forehead. He turned to Tommy. "Now, I believe, we're ready for baseball."

Mr. Watts walked Tommy home. When they got there, Tommy said, "Wait here for a minute. I want to give you something."

He went into the house and came back a few minutes carrying two books on baseball. "Maybe you'll have a chance to read these before you go to bed tonight. They'll explain the rules of the game to you." He handed the books to Mr. Watts. "By the way, where do you sleep?"

"I'm sorry, I can't give out any information on that subject. Thank you for the books. I'll study them before the next game."

"It's on Saturday. That gives you two days to learn the game. Things won't be so confusing to you then. We can do it," Tommy said with confidence.

"All right. We'll meet by the brook after school tomorrow. Good-by and good luck." Tommy stood on his porch and watched Mr. Watts climb the hill. "I wonder if he sleeps in a tree," Tommy thought, and started to laugh out loud.

The next afternoon Tommy taught Mr. Watts everything he knew about baseball. Mr. Watts was able to answer all questions correctly.

"You're pretty smart," Tommy said. "It has taken me all my life to know the game,

and you learn it in one afternoon."

Mr. Watts laughed. "Yes, but I don't think I would be able to play it half as well as you. Have you been thinking about your wish?"

Tommy nodded. "I've almost decided. I'll tell you tomorrow."

As soon as school was out the next day, Tommy raced home and up the hill. He said the words and Mr. Watts appeared.

"Well, young man, what is your wish? Just remember that this is the last time we can change it."

"I understand," Tommy said, "and just be sure you understand it before you say, 'Wish granted'." Mr. Watts nodded. "What I wish is for my last wish to be canceled."

"Am I understanding you correctly?" Mr. Watts asked. "Your wish is that you wish to cancel the old wish. That means you won't have any wish."

"That's it exactly. I've thought it over and what I really want is to be just a good pitcher and I think I can do that on my own. After all, the season is just starting and I haven't really had a chance to prove myself. All those wishes got in the way." Tommy brushed his hair back from his face. "Even after that perfect game I didn't feel right. If I do it on my own, I'm sure I'll feel better even if we lose."

"Wish granted. And I must say it was a pretty good last wish."

"Before you go, Mr. Watts, I want to say thanks. And do you suppose we could see each other every once in a while even though I don't have any more wishes?"

"I wish that could be possible," Mr. Watts said, and then started to laugh. "Now look at who is wishing." He became serious again. "I wasn't going to tell you, but I'm being transferred to Japan. My supervisor says there are to be no more wishes for this area. Just when I was beginning to learn and like the game of baseball."

Tommy offered his hand. "I'm sorry to see you leave, but next to the United States Japan is the biggest baseball country."

"You don't say," Mr. Watts rubbed his hands together. "Well, then, I really must be going. Good-by and good luck."

GREGG PRESS CHILDREN'S LITERATURE SERIES
ANN A. FLOWERS AND PATRICIA C. LORD, *Editors*